# DAUGHTERS
# OF OSHUN

## AFRO-CUBAN REFLECTIONS IN INWOOD
## MANHATTAN, NEW YORK.

### THERESA C. GAYNORD

Follow us at www.transcendentzeropress.org

ISBN:978-1-946460-68-4

"I don't like constant gore in horror. I like the subtle kind of horror, the intelligent horror that seeps into your soul and stays with you because it makes you question everything about existence and the human experience all at once. That to me, is the scariest horror. It reclaims the otherworldly pandemonium that is palpable and relentless. The one we all fear."

Theresa C. Gaynord

A child hears his own voice
among the trees
 speaking to him.
What does it ask?
The blistering atoms of reclusivity–
 they offer senses the eternity
where rivers meet.


Dustin Pickering

# CONTENTS

# AFRICA

In El Monte-The Wood, loas known as Iwa roam and speak spontaneously among a fortress of trees housed by flowing rivers that breach the divide between humans and the divine. What remains intact has been extended by the practitioners who serve them via oral traditions, songs, dances, symbols and rituals, as a form of service; intoxicating, secret, yet not easily embraced.

A case of loaves and fishes, shackles and reinforcements washed down by ocean waves, displace them into the obscure, with no apology for the lack of hospitality. Hardly their fault, but the spirits will not warrant them peace on a quiet summer's eve nor will they offer any exemptions to the curses that shatter the veil at guitar-wielding Spaniards who maintain plantations, replacing the beliefs of the Yoruba with elements of Catholicism by force, while fancy dinners are served on terraces under lamplights. Even those from the priestly class who possess the knowledge and wisdom of Ifa' will not be spared. Between myth and actuality, internal and external struggles, and the ceremonial significance of constellations, nature will nullify any imposed authority. The spirits, constantly in motion, always between things, forever evolving, forever on the move, contradicting, blessing, fearless, secret, based in solid roots, order and chaos, survive nonetheless. With limits and without, they talk and divulge immutable truths in a tangled language of meters and rhymes, that many look to for clarification. The crux of it all in the interpretation.

Mama Della grew up behind palm groves

    In Africa

  where the women danced

      and toms-toms beat

        rattling mangos off trees

        In Africa

where lips were sweet

and spirits kissed

and juju men

catered to deep

Rivers

In Africa

and blessed

drowned

little

Girls

of Oshun.

# UNDER THE GOLDEN SUN

Under the golden sun the soul begins to sing with false visions of safety,
as worlds appear and disappear into tributaries feeding large rivers. Many
lives are lived in the provisional world. And the self, invisible as it is, rein-
vents all and thrives, as cabildos surge in abundance. Cabildos, where the
ritual dances of African nations keep their faith alive. A compromise if you
will, to alleviate tensions between masters and slaves.


Why are you afraid? Is this not where the waters are?
A dream ended and started, began and exited in secret.
Is that not what the sea is, perhaps an illusion?
How sweet our music, alone in our grief.
   Oh Mother Oshun, can you hear us?
   Oh Mother Oshun our eyes have lost
   their footing.
   The earth grieves with us.
   When I awoke, I saw your children
         crying
          real
          tears
          of
         blood.
          We
            are
             not
               safe.
                Like
                a
                  kite
                   taken
                   away.

# TOM-TOMS

Repetitions beat with emotions in the balm of a summer night. There is desire mixed with loneliness that the wind carries like a kite. Lucumi rhythms apprentice themselves to the echoes of the Yoruba, burning with the insights given and received by the voices of the spirits who have answered the invocations. Dark predictions rise from within to the beat of the drums. Seven will die, a bride in white will become ill, a child is blessed. Rain pours as rituals are made and symbols are drawn for the lost and the remembered. Servants, in a kind of dream or trance, become small as the spirits appear on their backs at dawn. The mounting, an acquittal, an absolution, that moves and speaks like a sleepwalker,

wanting nothing
asking for nothing

yet in compliance to the great distance between the beats, and the fire of a gaze that sees inside the soul.

Night blooming flowers covered in evening stars
blossom from a limitless world.
The waters rise with the sounds of
taps, music over an
open sea.
Drums
a little softer,
a little louder,
more
plangent,
reclaim,
reenter,
bewitching
devotions
and
dreams.

In time,

under palm grove moons and the Orishas-Olodumare's eldest children blessed with a portion of her ache,' scattered bits and pieces of vibrational energy over the Earth and over humanity while Olodumare went on to create other universes-other worlds. The nights can split the world in two and blend them together making one golden crown where sweet freedom lies imprisoned in burning embers and danger is near, and voices grow silent though brave, like a forgotten day that is somewhere around but not yet found. Within the crossroads, windows of Roman Catholicism and Yoruba beliefs and practices intermixed and coexisted as their evolution moved forward on a river's edge. And vats of fire elevated the scattered dead into everything bare, cold, receptive, behind a bend of trees, behind the glare on windows, the words spoken and the blue of heaven.

A bird can fly, skirt the palm groves,
reflect its sorrow, its violent edge
against a full moon.

His hunger felt
among the summoning,
his wanting, driven
by severed wings
ashen and sorted
for the battle
and departure.

life wi...

terminate

its story.

And it will sleep, so the winds can awaken!

# THE CAMP

Visions emerge with lightning, done with speed and soul. The grass grows below old trees while the wooden palo-the stick, points to earthworms, framed by wire-like vines. The dandelion, summer's cotton, drifts, carrying with it the wishes of those who touched and blew it free. In the camp, Mama Della is a priestess, and Oriki Damilola, a priest. As young adults they were ordained under La Regla Lucumi' receiving the mysteries of Eleggua', Obatala', Oshun, Yemaya', and Chango'. The African way. Mama Della's tutelary is Oya' and Oriki Damilola's is Aggayu'. They move towards the night and do not question the steps they take. It begins in silence, a dedication, a calling that pierces flesh. The sun glides over them in the morning, as do flowing waters. Their skin that glistens, a mirror, to the burning wheel of time that passes gently over them, without lamentations.

The sky shimmers the birches, dark wood rises again.
The mourning dove holds its song,
while trailing leaves skim the surface
of waters,
spitting up
waves
like the sands of time
personified
into a
different
world.

In the camp the juju man is a priest.

He caters to deep Rivers

far from Africa
and blesses
drowned

little girls of Oshun.

# CANALS

When floating down canals, keep your extremities to yourself. Do not touch the waters, do not taste the air, do not look for spiritual signs, do not listen to gentle waves, do not smell the muck nor the sun on sweat. Work compulsively, in practical terms, eyes down to common ground. A general rule you must not break, work compulsively, that is your fate. Be subtle with your courage, and pray to their God. Knee bend and head expressed in nod.

Eleggua-St. Anthony owner of the crossroads,
 little trickster, impish child
  wearer of red and black,
   like a picture book moon,
   a golden sun,
    we witness you,
     we pay homage
    via church bells
      and a network
       of
        canals.

Ogun-St.Peter, oh mighty warrior, divine blacksmith,
 your weapons brand the thorns that await
     the turning.

Ochosi-St. Norbert, divine hunter, in your accuracy
   stalk the hills gently
   for your people.
   Offer blind justice
     and a triumphal end

to all suffering.

Oko-St. Isidore, under the stars you give birth and life.
Fertile earth surrenders to your touch.
Crops and black earth
grow
under your
direction.
The great mother
looks on with

pleasure.


Olokun, the depths of the seas are your domain.
In the abyss, does the heart continue to beat?
Is your gift in the deep waters,
the closeness of

death?


Babalu' Aye'-St. Lazarus, will you heal your people from all illness?
Our souls travel together, hunger for the familiarity of
being pain free.
Concerning

darkness,

we are frail in it.

Malaise

surrounds all beings.
We
Are
Not
Immortal.

Ibji-St. Cosme, St. Damian, divine twins in one. Oshun gave birth to you,

whirling in the blackness of night. She was called a witch! And so you
were rejected. Oya' came forth instead, as your adoptive mother!

And in low bushes you played.
And in the heaviest woods all was
still.
One boy dressed in red. One girl dressed in blue. She,
the elder of the two.

Obatala'-Our Lady of Mercy, the eldest of the Orishas. You journeyed with
us. Owner of the white cloth, king of peace and logic. Part male, part
female.
Silent in your work.

You walk and guide
in afternoon gardens,
where the sun bursts with gratitude
and all creatures hide a prayer
on your high altar!

Obba-St. Catherine of Sienna, Chango's wife, ensnared him by witchcraft.
Beside the earth's edge, a cemetery, a transformation took place. A return
to power, to sharpen her will. A homely rendition, a missing left ear, a
headwrap to cover the wound.
Wax dissolves.
The sun bleeds
obliterating light.
Return to me
She asks,
on a

dangerous hill.

Oya'-St. Theresa, with multicolored skirt, fierce warrior and owner of the cemetery gates, you stole the secret of slinging lightning from Chango', Iku'-death even fears you!

Machetes rattle, cut through
traveling stone
and brush,
wisk by tendrils
and vine.

Hissing as air burns.

Yegua'-Our Lady of Montserrat, adorned in pink and burgundy, chaste and pure, violated by Chango', residing at the bottom of a grave. Death and decomposition, the dying process as the moon rises, picking clean sheaves of skin,

Bound

To

Eternal

Rest.

A

Harvest

And

A

Pestilence.

The hills darken around surrounding the expiration, their hands extended

In

Payment.

Aggayu'-Saint Christopher, Chango''s father. Orisha of the volcano, fer-
ryman across the great river. Empty is your ear against wrinkled lips that
long to hear the truth. The desert carries charred fragments of memories,
while your double headed ax with curved double handle shakes,
so
many
　　free
　　　　now

　　　　　　　　　　　　　　　　　　　　　　　traveling home

the aroma of sweat consistent with the variation of

　　　　　　　　　　　　　　　　　　　　　　　their daily
move.
Far from Africa

Oshun, Orisha of love and beauty. Your sweetness touches young girls,
mirrors and imparts beyond wisdom, your bearing gifts.

Ghosts of child brides

　　　　　　　too clairvoyant

　　　　　　　　　　　　　　　　reads the patterns

at the bottom

of dainty

teacups

She will kiss you,

then bury you

under a mango tree

Yemaya', Mother of all living things. Queen of the oceans.

The waters of sadness call out to you, Mother of all Orishas!

Salt of concession and betrayal

Your children now concubines

and courtesans

of slavery.

Mercantile trade in the port

of Spain.

Chango', Saint Barbara, Orisha of lightning, thunder and fire.

Sacred bata' drums

proliferate the room

Bearing

The

Scars

of

Emancipation.

Orunmila, Saint Frances of Assisi, Orisha of divination,

Babalawos bring the offering of sugar,

Immaculate sight

Glittering like a diamante

Comfortable in their

working.

All stories are theirs, born of pain, merged in voice and tradition.

A method of memory, a balanced sentence,

artifacts to the gods and their people

where forced edges blur hurt

inventive

approaching a dream.

# BEADS OF BRONZE

In Cuba, way down a deserted street,
a sidewalk is narrow, its location,
historic.


Brushes of pink and white aura a church tower,
glowing naturally in the brilliance of
rain.

Uniform appearance of droplets,
keep their pitch and pace,
as if on an errand,
not of this world.


Way back on a cobblestone corner,
gently placed on the ground,
an altar to San Lazaro offers hope and healing,
outside the front door
of a home.


The collar of his purple cloak bent upwards to the Heavens,

encased in glass,

against the neon light

falling,

dormant, yet all consuming.

Its projections, like beads of bronze, defy explanation.

# UNDER A CONTINUOUS DREAM

In Hialeah, Detective Rudy Garcia (criminal investigation division),
    follows the finest convex curves of blue,
                that blister like open wounds in the night sky.

                        Rain and lightning, ruffle thunder, a sure sign
Santa Barbara is near.


Bellowing wildlife, trees and nature, speak though chemical air.

The detective blesses himself. Invoking Aggayu' for protection.

                        Something is amiss.

Bad things happen this way. With a first sign. An indication of what is to
come.

Light then darkness patterns the sky, each their own way, leaving an
imprint. Some say it's a miracle from the divine, while others believe the
devil is cascading down to earth, flapping open the gates of hell for all to
enter.

Detective Rudy Garcia has a reoccurring dream about just that.
        Various devils holding up the earth, as demons move around it,
                growing larger in the expanse of time.

# PAINTED SKIN

In Hialeah, Jose Fuente drums in the safety of his garage while the rain accompanies the rhythm, heavy with soot and soil on the tin roof.
He is paying homage to the spirits.
His gift, as the sounds merge with Mother Earth.

Jose often says that the soul could never really be understood or penetrated, and one can only touch its outer layer. He understands things. Like when the sun settles on the shoulder of the road with hints of gold, it is time passing by in the construct of a wrong turn.

Painted skin chronicles emptiness even though it beckons protection, offering, and a warrior nature akin to the Orishas.

There is a bridge before Jose, and a woman is waiting for him on the other side.

There's a rumor about his impending death.

The drum between his legs,

a stab at preservation.

Heads are down and blood is in the waters.

Melancholy carries his pleas.

He will survive some, before he grows weak from battle.

# THE LAST GLANCE

There's a woman. Tall, pale, elegant looking at one time.
You can tell by the way she moves and carries herself.
Classy,

like an old movie star.

She holds a cigarette in her right hand, and wears Oshun beads
around her neck.

Her rent is paid on time,

and she speaks with dead politeness.

Just nice enough.

Locals call her, The Lady of Hialeah.

And they light candles outside the front porch of her home,

sing hymns of protection

both a warning and invocation.

The neighbors and The Lady of Hialeah, negotiate her life ceaselessly,

with ceremony,

and instrumentality,

as the spirits oversee.

They all know her fate.

In the symbiosis of her home, a stranger enters.

A whisper to the angels brush her lips,

as the wound around her neck gapes open,

spilling blood.

The first to die

beneath the seven winds of change.

The last glance, disappearing over the edge of the sun and moon,

an in between place

of flesh and growth.

She was far more than the sum of her spilled blood,

far more than the breath seeping

from her lips.

She was a daughter of Oshun.

Full of ache',

descendant of the ancestors with one hundred thousand names.

A favored child

to sacred bloodlines

and connected knowledge of Divine power.

# SENSING DEATH

In Cuba, way down a deserted street,

a family cries for their own,

The Lady of Hialeah.

Under that Cuban roof,

instinctual moves heal.

There are low frequency waves of other planes,

allowing spirits to be transported

to a place of perceivable emotion.

Here, she is longed for

and remembered.

When The Lady of Hialeah arrives home,

she will be draped in a yellow dress.

Gold around her neck,

Gold bangles on her wrists.

River waters will caress her skin,

one last time.

Flowing hair will mirror her beauty in the waters.

Those who loved her cry each day by the river's edge,

longing

for all they have lost.

Herbs burn on charcoal,

and on candles,

while black tourmaline removes negative energy.

A spiritual repertoire,

for those sensing death.

# THE PASSING TIDES

Here, in the mind is the tedium of despair,

where passing tides blend among persistent rain.

Limping down the long hallway of his home,

Detective Rudy Garcia holds himself up with sheer will,

hoping to disappear

in twilight.

They get in his head!

THE DEAD.

And he can't quite shut them up.

Their bodies are pressed against warm cement,

remembered

and forgotten,

just as the sun goes down

and the moon hasn't risen,

and hell exists somewhere in the distance, under an old oak tree.

# BUZZARDS OVERHEAD

Jose Fuente works with brujos, witches, of all kind,
for all types of goals and ends.

He smokes cigars, plays the drums and overindulges on

RUM!

The Cuban people of Hialeah say, he holds the mysteries among all brujos,
the key to the cemetery gates.

They often refer to him as The Baron, for this reason alone.

Jose, The Baron has the unusual ability to command
many spirits.

And his power extends across the distances of time and space.

Something he personally likes to keep secret.

Just like the spirits, Jose, The Baron, is like the wind and air.

He is constantly in motion,

active,

watching,

summoning.

Death is all around him,

in him.

He is ill and dying.

Every minute that goes by,

a mini death occurs.

It has its own reputation and magic, death.

The people of Hialeah know this too.

It happened the minute they fled Cuba.

It's in their lineage.

Ancient.

Filled with African invocations, Our Fathers and Hail Marys.

Death is everywhere,

all at once,

one step away

from life.

Jose Fuente will not die today.

With drum between his legs,

he will survive some,

before he grows weak from battle.

Calista and Manuel Sanchez were teachers from Hialeah.

They were best known for their ability to undo hexes, black magic,

amarres-magical ties.

In a dream once, Calista learned how to do cleansings.

The African way.

Colors of old often reveal themselves to sleep,

among skeletons

that grasp your hands firmly,

while singing lullabies.

Calista and Manuel see themselves in the structure

of these colors of old,

the continuity

of actual effort, of cause and effect where no two are alike.

This is how they lived

and how they died.

Waiting,

checking for the sun to look away,

while buzzards fly overhead

and mourners pack into the funeral home,

and the organ plays,

in resonant air,

and memory becomes

a murdered acquaintance.

They are the second and third to die.

# THAT STILL MOMENT WHEN LIFE STOPS

Death becomes more and more at ease

with the serpent.

Santa Marta The Dominator, pierces its side.

There is cold rage in the penetration.

A vessel by day,

a weapon by night,

She is invoked on the eve of a wedding.

The African Way.

Her ebb and flow like that of a snake, a twining river,

humped and heavy

offering aid and protection

to overcome all difficulties,

for the happy couple.

The bride, a daughter of Oshun',

moves with the cycles of the sun,

and the spirit that imbues her very constitution.

She grows and thrives, bears burdens and is faithful

to her nature.

She is both the north

star and the burning sun,

African moon and gold-dust

that murmurs,

a split tree,

and trepid air

of the Seven African Powers-

Las Siete Potencias Africanas!

She-The Bride is the favored child.

The Untouchable One!

Her wedding brings everyone together,

on a mid-morning afternoon.

A reprieve from the aching deaths of their own,

the murders and spilled blood

of the innocent.

When she takes her vows, her voice echoes to the mountains,

beyond any concrete place,

beyond time.

Her groom accompanies her love,

a reciprocal;

and spiritual return

to Africa.

Jose Fuente will drum at the binding ceremony,

while The Bride hugs her spiritual brother,

her face, heavy with the sight.

Jose is dread.

The outline of the trees outside have spoken.

The sunlight dims,

just for a moment.

The Bride pauses in mid hug.

Between them is sleep

and restlessness.

He knows that she knows.

And the sunlight appears once again.

It's another time, in another world.

The Bride bound by a code of silence.

without compromise,

the African way,

becomes ill.

Sometimes innate knowledge can be brutal.

And sometimes, love and survival bleed as one,

equally.

It's like finding a beautiful flower in the dust,

only to watch it die.

Even for a daughter of Oshun, who knows the soul rides on a black winged hawk,

over stretches of mountains

and rivers, it's hard to let go.

Sickness enters the pit of her stomach,

and she vomits,

amid ruins reminiscent of Africa
and Cuba,

where the palm offers its leaves to the wind,

and a High Priestess offers her flesh to her groom.

In that still moment when life stops.

# CELEBRATION

In Hialeah, on a day where the fog is thick with mists

of heavy rain, a child is born.

Toms-Toms beat at her arrival

while her mother falls weak from the

loss of blood.

There's a slight red birthmark around her neck,

and the practitioners present,

gasp at the sight.

Jose Fuente stops the drumming.

Darkness falls in the parameters of his mind.

The child's beginning,

his end.

The soul knows itself!

It reasons with the sky in its salt and wind travel.

Detective Rudy Garcia knows too.

As do the spiritual people of Hialeah.

The babe is a child of Oshun, full of ache, and the reincarnation of

The Lady of Hialeah.

She is blessed in celebration and culture,

the African Way.

On the third day of her birth the ocean waves are wild,

and nature's voices, buoyant with significance.

# AN ANCHOR ON HER BREAST

The ocean greets the Blessed Child of Hialeah. Yemaya greets her sister
Oshun

in the mighty waters.

The sands turn,

with water sprouts,

emitting a sweet perfume.

Chocolate sparks fill the radium sunlight,

reflecting in ocean spills

of gold.

Cassiopeia drifts from the thrones of night,

as fire and anchor

lay on their breasts, sprung from the dark blood of their power.

# TATTOO ON HER BACK

In Cuba, way down a deserted street,

news of The Blessed Child

bring joy.

The moon is orange, full and resting on the surface of the ocean,

latching itself back and forth with the gentle waves that mirror it.

But the tips are like blades,

stabbing the scene.

There is blood in the waters.

And it is rising with the current.

Detective Rudy Garcia tastes blood in his mouth.

Fever violates, invades his physical and spiritual body.

He screams in his sleep.

Even though he is retired from the police department,

they will not let him rest,

the dead.

The spirits are vast,

tongue lit

and chaotic,

like the pages of this book.

Like the Grus-the crane stars, sacred to the messenger gods, where good luck and longevity reign.

Detective Rudy Garcia wanders in between worlds,

the Cuban way.

Lost in a monomaniacal chain that won't give way,

even after his rejection of it.

The seven winds just like the seven African powers,

will not let go of one of their own.

They will scavenge him from the earthly plane,

against his will

when nature disappears in its entirety,

and books of poetry are burned,

out of fear.

Like a history lesson to man,

a tattoo on the back of the neck,

a spin-off of the sea mist and sun,

a blessing

and curse.

She was found on the beach after a tropical storm.

Sea-weed covered her face and hair,

blood and sand decorated her body.

She was beautiful in death,

even as beads of blood cascaded down her legs in a straight line.

It was free flowing menstrual blood,

the cause of death, strangulation.

There are latent seascapes that come alive like art,

like the circumference of a sacred circle,

kept and desired

by its casting light of candles lit, the tattoo on her back

and the free flow of a woman menstruating.

She

is

the

fourth

to

die.

# A BIRD'S NEST

There's a gray house with blue doors in Hialeah.

In its interior, old Tereza arranges her porcelain elephants with upturned trunks in a row.

They bring good luck.

She has a red embroidered rug that has gotten smoky with age.

There's a symbolic bird's nest between her thighs,

representing her home and chastity.

It is said Old Tereza can either bless or curse you,

depending on her mood.

As a practitioner, she often uses discarded bird nests for spells, for witch-craft.

Discarded ones, because she never endangered the homes of nesting birds.

They became a symbol of her home of her devotion and sacrifice.

Charged eggs are given to the Daughters of Oshun for fertility.

Abandoned by youth,

she locks herself away.

Found weeks later by the stench that alerts neighbors.

Her breasts cut off, blood spilled all over her bedsheets,

all over her childhood blanket.

It is said the house is now haunted by her spirit.

Her ache' remaining in its abyss,

unable to be rented, bought or occupied.          She is the fifth to die.

# WHITE SHADOWS

Stoneways in Cuba are collapsing, crumbling with tons of garbage.

The houses have fallen to decay,

as clouds are scudding by blues, driven by winds.

What is and what was remains,

are modified in dust,

like creatures of comfort,

redistributed

by psychic powers

many don't understand.

Like a putrid acid

rancid with revenge,

and hellbent on violence.

White shadows are their own species of retribution.

Purity, peace and spiritual alignment walk with them;

Santeros, initiated with the seating of the god on their heads.

There is dedication and spiritual rebirth in their journey.

The rivers are lined with them.

There is protection offered,

as they honor their ancestors.

They walk with their heads down,

with colorful elekes-beaded necklaces around their necks, contrasting
Cuba's derelict collapse.

Maria Del Carmen Hernan was one of them. An initiate, living in Hialeah.

She was found among the dead leaves,

fallen from a mango tree.

Under the mango tree, diseased leaves and mango-rot puddle heavy rain.

Detective Rudy Garcia can see the image in his head,

and feels the pain in his heart.

He wants indifference.

He is retired after all.

The gift of sight is his cross.

His curse.

She-The Woman in White, is the sixth to die.

# THE OPPRESSED

The oppressed are always remembered,

even if our governments choose to forget them.

They gather under the eaves of spiritual days,

and stretch out against the skies where Orion's

moon, oversees the night.

The sadness leaves

and returns,

as lampshades

glow

and ache'

dissipates.

# TEMPLES OF GODS

La Regla Lucumi lives in her history,

in the temples of the gods

that intrudes dreams.

Even within Santeria there are many paths,

many different incarnations.

There are doorsteps you cannot enter,

hardships that must be endured,

and the ache' of the river

that must be imparted.

The many faces of Oshun are

everywhere.

In blessings, in birthright, in tradition, in song, dances, drums,

and in the sweet fluidity of the rivers.

She is the amniotic fluid that caresses and punishes,

the purveyor of love,

in the temples of gods.

# INWOOD DREAMS

Jose Fuente-The Baron of Hialeah sits cross-legged

in a sacred circle of blessed salt.

Cigar, various liquids and liquors, a rosary, candles

and silver bell,

the spiritual elements of the brujo are with him.

He feels tingling in his arms and legs

as he begins the ritual.

Different plants are rubbed through his shirtless body, up and down,

a cleansing and healing

like a surrender to warm light.

He smiles and dreams of peace,

deep peace,

the kind that makes you sleep where you wake up stronger,

more alive.

He controls the dead, Jose Fuentes does.

And he can remove them,

reverse any attacks,

revert them back to sender.

He has healed all kinds of hexes and physical ailments before.

All illnesses,

controlling life and death to buy someone more time on Earth.

His powers,

his blood sacrifices

have done the same for him,

brought him more time.

He can bring back lost lovers together,

or separate them.

Death can be used a number of ways,

but in the end,

a debt must be paid.

The African Way.

The Blessed Child and her family are moving out of Hialeah to Inwood Manhattan, New York.

She has now grown into her power,

a daughter of Oshun.

Even at five years old, her power has grown immensely.

The Baron sees her as a threat.

The move away from Hialeah will keep her safe.

Inwood in its innate nature,

can dismantle the dead,

and disconnect from them.

Winds like chimes mix there with nature's open space and natural incense.

The Hudson River, the conduit to it all against spiritual washes and baptisms.

It is where the alignment began,

quiet, introverted and stable,

with the Lenape people,

the original inhabitants of the land,

now called,

Inwood Hill Park in New York City.

Like the African people, they were also violently

displaced.

The Blessed Child, now of Inwood,

is the bruja of her sanctuary.

Far from Africa.   Far from Hialeah.

# INDIGENOUS

Detective Rudy Garcia feels a reprieve,

from the dead.

When something is of cosmic proportion,

like an earthquake,

or the death of an innocent,

he can always feel it coming,

seeing it as part of a wheel,

or cosmological message.

His reaction is always to fix the problem by removing the obstacle,

but Detective Rudy Garcia is old, and retired.

The world spills into the Earth, and the Earth allows distorted space in.

Life is too short,

too unfaithful,

like the tides of an ocean.

Here, indigenous travelers come and go as they please.

You can sense them in the morning air,
in and around the trees and rivers

and marshes.

The beat of their drums escalating,

warning.

We are bonded to them,

and to the night.

They are the forces of the present, illuminating downtown buildings in
Manhattan, and oceans of devotees in Hialeah.

One day, all will disappear under a benign invasion,

passing into essences that brush with open seas,

guards of heat and windscape,

that affect the foraging behavior of seabirds.

Indigenous edges pervade,

they serve for now,

but will soon leave,

swallowed up,

by the hands

of time.

# DYCKMAN STREET

The Blessed Child feels at home on Dyckman Street.

It is the way the air speaks there,

like a mist over water falls,

a salutation

from

one powerful force

to another.

When it rains on Dyckman Street, it is a spiritual alert to the

life art,

a destined call,

to the remnants of timeless moments, that disappear and reappear in an aesthetic instant.

# THE A TRAIN

The A train maintains a witch's dignity with ease.

It is alive and dead,

like a metaphor

for an organized movement of people,

freedom seekers in the beauty of distress,

that ride the rails,

where vanity is its name and hell swears

forgiveness,

over smut, grime, rhymes and blasphemies.

A subterranean, witty seesaw of praise, flattery and held shame,
going nowhere.                                    Far from home.

# NAGLE'S 1 TRAIN

The rails repress and indulge the flight.

On a mural at Nagle's #1 train stop, someone scribbles Apollo's spite.

Ripen spirits enlighten,

thundering beneath soil.

Each journey becoming the spleen of a new book,

a rushing host in rout,

of an hour,

where trampled men groan with pain,

in unison with screeching steel.

A repeated cry, to the mustering squadrons in a clattering car.

# TRENDS

The soul is the body's guest,

withered dry by clay-cold lips

                    that do not speak.

Poisonous weeds burn and trend with the owl who watches,

                                        from a dead man's
grave.

There's art to all that trends,

                    and to all that tends.

Things are different in New York City.

                    Santeria is different in New York City.

Far from Africa. Far from Cuba. And far from Hialeah.

# GEOLOGY

Ophiolites are not spun when life is done, but preserved in mountain belts.

When exposed along a riverbed,

the wandering geologic feature, the rocks,

found on ancient ocean floors,

slave to fate,

like bones upon the soul's delivery,

swell ,

past all sleep.

They wake up eternally, betrothed to the river that has cut through the belt revealing and exposing it, as mermaid's sing that it has cleft the devil's hoof.

# THE CHURCH AND THE SCHOOL

The Blessed Child attends the local church and school where she is told
that anyone who beholds God shall never taste death's misery.

How sweet and fair that seems to be.

Wonderfully sweet and fair.

When night comes, she hunts and tries catching a falling star,

a strange thing to do for most,

but she was borne of strange things and strange sights,

most, too invisible to see beyond this monstrous world.

And the shores and surrounding seas, moist in their vows,

beneath the watery floor of an ocean bed,
shepherds woeful lullabies, to this Daughter of
Oshun.

# THE CLOISTERS

There are lingering blooms, never delayed, laboring beneath spreading trees,

circled by shade.

The Blessed Child wanders the Cloisters and its grounds,

innocent in her youth,

but not ignorant of her gifts.

Murmurs fluctuate on grass grown high,

informing of a seventh death.

Beneath an evening-moon,

when the grass is wet with rain-drops,

distant waters will roar among melancholy drum beats.

# FORT TRYON PARK

Thin smoke without flame is a hearthside ease coming from the apartment buildings that line Fort Tryon Park.

The Blessed Child lives in one,

as cuckoo clocks chime once every hour.

Meek and mild creatures of the park,

crown a winter day,

while the faces of children, blue and bleak,

play.

Little mittens fit small hands as the sun settles on red cheeks,

only for a

moment.

White flakes fall,

muffling and stifling childhood screams.

The clouds travel,

from the frosty heavens,

as beauty labors, greeting a new day in.

Fort Tryon Park is a world in and of itself,

charged,

with its own energy,

with its own spirituality,

the last light of nature never spent,

and earth's sweet being,

in Eden's garden.

# COMMUNITY GARDENS

Jose Fuente walks along the community gardens of a nearby park in Hialeah, with elected silence.

His nostrils breathe in the lusty air,

perfumed by flower and soil.

He thinks of The Blessed Child,

the life she has in front of her,

and the way his life is dwindling like twinkling foam,

far away from Africa.

Far Away from Cuba.

The reprieve given to him by the spirits,

is over.                    He cries realizing his fate.              Disheartened.

His protest is also a prophecy.

And he will touch it again in

spirit;

immortality.

There will be kingdoms with kings and queens,

and he will share their

space,

rising to judge the world.

He will become the hangman,

upon the air,

and his agony will pass.

In his death,

he will bless, drowned little girls of Oshun.

# THE HOSPITAL

The spiritual people of Hialeah are holding a vigil for Jose Fuente, The Baron, outside Miami Dade hospital.

He

      is

          dying.

They offer comfort to console,

          grace, in a lonely place.

Upon his lips not a word is spoken.

          Nor a sigh,

as orderlies scrub the doors and floors,

      with potent disinfectant, and clattering pails.

# SAXOPHONE

The pounding waves of the ocean reverberate with the sound of a saxo-
phone.

A mellow and strong range fills the coast-
line,

fading then returning like a spiritual sign that confesses in its confusion.

This is where passion lives and dies,

in the familiar waters,

that strike and fall,

a faint foretelling,

hushed by whispers that quiver down to shore,

an intoxicable cure to beauty's lore
and its creations.

# PIANO BLUES

The Blessed Child of Oshun sits at her piano.

She conducts a summer melody for
Oshun and her tutelary, Oya'.

Passersby and spiritual High Priests and Priestesses from every order, stop
to hear her play.

She smells of mango trees, woods, and frozen lakes.

She has promises to keep,

fences to mend,

homages to pay.

The sun spills from her pores,

mending

time,

the African and Cuban way,

beyond the hills, beyond the mountains,

and waterfalls,

beyond the rivers and their banks heavy with boulders.

# CROCODILE ART

Nile crocodiles can be aggressive,

however,

they are sacred.

☐hey carry offerings to the goddess Olosa.

Many, are

selected by priests,

under sky gatherings.

☐hey are fed and sheltered.

Worshipers sing under falling rain,

under portable amulets and offerings that,

bind and stretch through many portals.

The crocodiles gather together too,

observing the worshipers like oval blobs

bobbing up and down in the waters.

The foliage enshrouds,

paired off by black circles of smoke,

and drum beats.

The final circle back to the sun,

back to Africa,

free

as a people.

Sisters and brothers of survival.

# DOWN BY THE WATERFALLS

My name is Mari, The Blessed Child.

I roam the pages of this book,

the streets of Hialeah,

the cosmos of Inwood,

and the living spiritual world of Africa and Cuba.

I am a woman now full of Ache'.

Mama Della and Oriki Damilola are here with me too.

They, like me, are visible in the smoky air, the slight breeze that drifts,

baring all;

eternal.

I decorate myself in yellow, and gesture in beauty.

I am a child of Oshun,

untouchable,

unstoppable.

In me is art, tradition, homage, sacrifice and song.

Gifts of sunflowers, honey, fruits and liquors honor me.

I am generous with my own.

And I chronicle my life with white intentions,

transforming them,

into black compensation.

I am Mari, The Blessed Child,

and Daughter of Oshun!

I would like to thank my publishers Dustin Pickering and Z. M. Wise  for their patience, professionalism and for their diligence in publishing this book. I appreciate them very much!

Cuba libre! Patria y Vida!

## The Reviews

DAUGHTERS OF OSHUN-AFRO-CUBAN REFLECTIONS IN IN-WOOD MANHATTAN, NEW YORK by Theresa C. Gaynord is a unique storytelling through poetry of the intermingling of tribal beliefs and Catholicism with a horror undertone. Her prose is rhythmic and paints a vivid canvas with colours of Afro-Cuban culture. The horror draws on your intellect to bring dread. This work is highly unique and very well written. I highly recommend.-Jeff Ashley- Author.

"Gaynord sets out to display poetry telling a story. I was immediately pulled in. The story is there. The history, the compassion, and the revelation is in black and white. I was exposed to things I never knew!" -- Phillip Tomasso, author of My Weekly Devotional for Daily Struggles

# ABOUT THE AUTHOR

Theresa C. Gaynord is an occult expert, international author, and former teacher- Who's Who Among America's Teachers 1993 Award.
Her books are available for purchase in the UK and US. Check amazon. com
This is Theresa's seventh book publication.

www.ingramcontent.com/pod-product-compliance
Lightning Source LLC
Chambersburg PA
CBHW072017170626
46813CB00005B/2175